A Scarf and a Half

'A Scarf and a Half'
An original concept by Amanda Brandon
© Amanda Brandon

Illustrated by Catalina Echeverri

Published by MAVERICK ARTS PUBLISHING LTD

Studio 3A, City Business Centre, 6 Brighton Road,

Horsham, West Sussex, RH13 5BB

© Maverick Arts Publishing Limited August 2015

+44 (0)1403 256941

A CIP catalogue record for this book is available at the British Library.

ISBN 978-1-84886-177-0

www.maverickbooks.co.uk

This book is rated as: Orange Band
The original picture book text for this story has been modified
by the author to be an early reader.

A Scarf and a Half

by Amanda Brandon

illustrated by
Catalina Echeverri

Granny Mutton loved to knit.

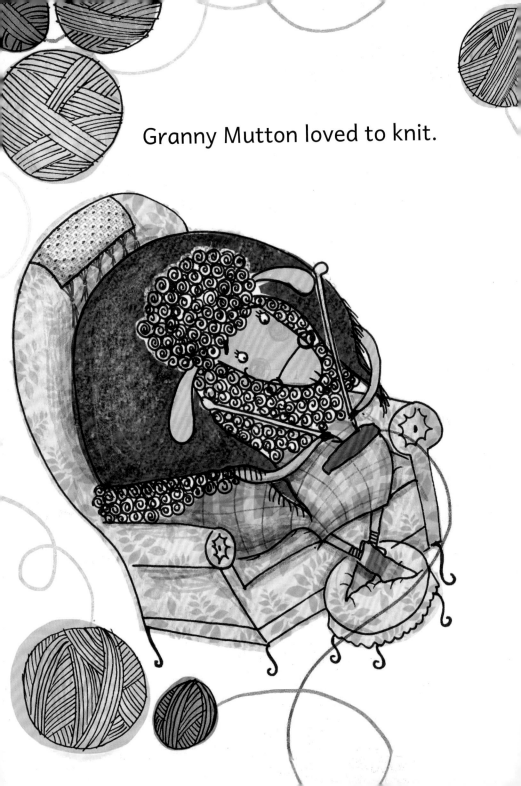

She knitted blankets for baby lambs, woolly hats for chilly rams, and snug socks for sheep-dogs.

She made a rainbow scarf for

Little Lionel's birthday.

It grew and grew and grew.

"Stop, Granny, stop!" everyone said.

"That's not a scarf, that's a scarf and a half!"

So Granny Mutton stopped.

She gave the scarf to Little Lionel
with her love.

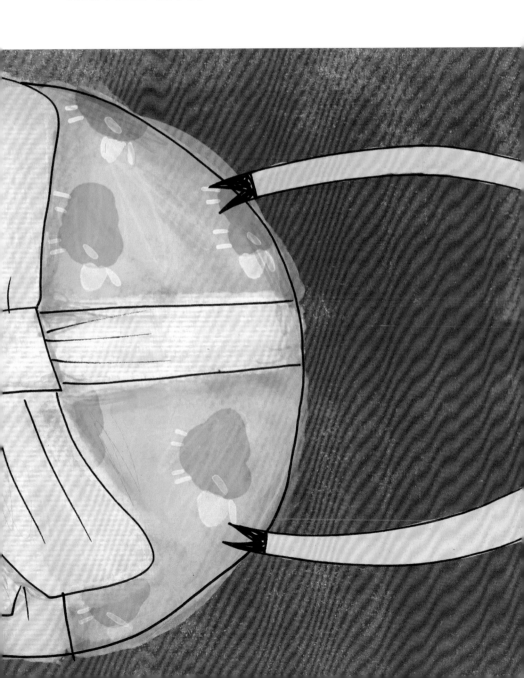

Little Lionel was excited. He thought the present was a football.

He ripped open the paper but...

...it was just a scarf.

"You can't have a laugh with a scarf,"

he said crossly.

But Granny Mutton couldn't hear him.

Little Lionel's scarf was so long that he tripped and landed in a muddy puddle.

SPLAT!

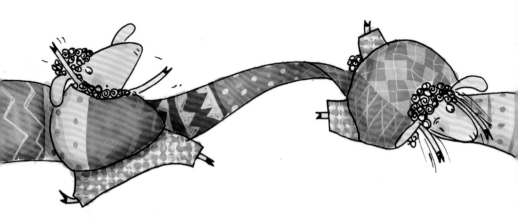

He tried skipping with the scarf
but he kept falling over.

"It's no good! You can't have a laugh
with a scarf," he said. He threw his
present away.

Lionel's friend Bleater found the scarf.

"That's a scarf and a half!" he said.

He turned the scarf into a swing.

Lionel and Bleater swung high and low.

Rocky the sheep-dog came by.

"That's not a scarf," he woofed.

"That's a scarf and a half!"

He tied the scarf to his cart and took Lionel and Bleater for a ride.

Little Lionel started to cheer up.

More friends came to see his

amazing present.

"That's not a scarf, that's a scarf and a half!" they all said. They PULLED and PULLED in a crazy tug of war.

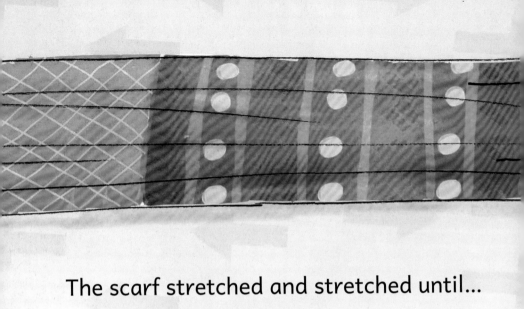

The scarf stretched and stretched until...

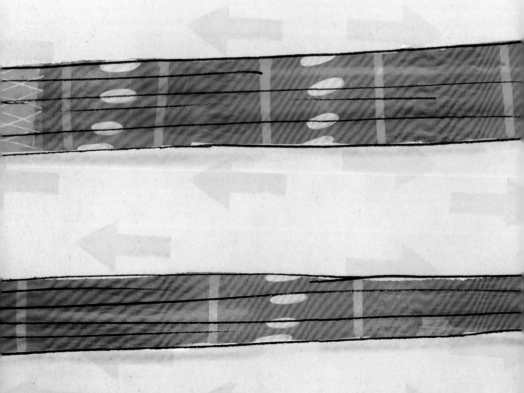

it was twice as long.

PING! Everyone let go, and landed in a

HIGGLEDY PIGGLEDY pile.

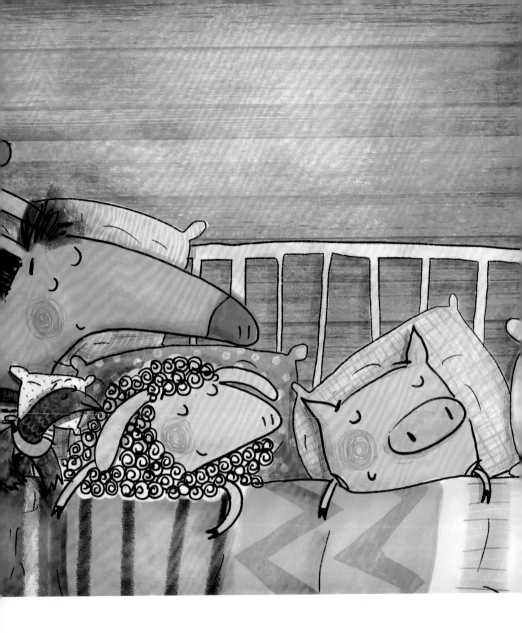

Later, the friends snuggled down at
Granny Mutton's house.

"I've got a scarf and a half," Lionel said.

"And I've got a Granny and a half, too!"

Quiz

1. What does Little Lionel think his present is?
a) A toy car
b) A game
c) A football

2. What game does Lionel and his friends play?
a) Hop scotch
b) Tug of war
c) Hide and seek

3. What animal is Rocky?
a) A sheep-dog
b) A sheep
c) A donkey

4. What colour is Lionel's scarf?

a) Pink

b) Orange and blue

c) Rainbow coloured

5. What does Bleater turn the scarf into?

a) A catapult

b) A swing

c) A bandage

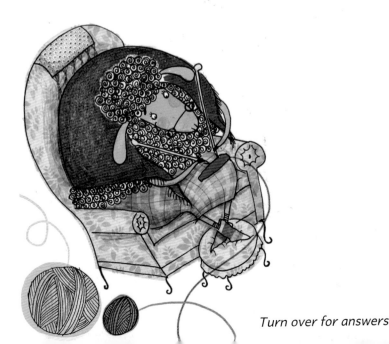

Turn over for answers

Maverick Early Readers

Our early readers have been adapted from the original picture books so that children can make the essential transition from listener to reader.

All of these books have been book banded to the industry standard and edited by a leading educational consultant.

Green

Early Reader
Yuck! said the Yak
by Alex English Illustrated by Emma Levey
ISBN 978-1-84886-176-3

Orange

Early Reader
The **Black** and **White Club**
by Alice Hemming Illustrated by Kimberley Scott
ISBN 978-1-84886-179-4

Early Reader
A **Scarf** and a **Half**
by Amanda Brandon
Illustrated by Catalina Echeverri
ISBN 978-1-84886-177-0

Turquoise

Early Reader
PREPOSTEROUS RHINOCEROS
by Tracy Gunaratnam Illustrated by Marta Costa
ISBN 978-1-84886-180-0

Early Reader
HOCUS POCUS DIPLODOCUS
by Steve Howson
Illustrated by Kate Daubney
ISBN 978-1-84886-178-7

Quiz Answers:

1c, 2b, 3a, 4c, 5